Mary Poppins

in the Kitchen

Also by P. L. Travers

MARY POPPINS

MARY POPPINS COMES BACK

MARY POPPINS OPENS THE DOOR

MARY POPPINS IN THE PARK

MARY POPPINS FROM A TO Z

P. L. TRAVERS

Mary Poppins
in the Kitchen

**A Cookery Book
with a Story**

With drawings by Mary Shepard

HARCOURT, INC.

Orlando Austin New York San Diego Toronto London

www.HarcourtBooks.com

Culinary Consultant: Maurice Moore-Betty

First published 1975

Library of Congress Cataloging-in-Publication Data
Travers, P. L. (Pamela Lyndon), 1899–1996.
Mary Poppins in the kitchen: a cookery book with a story/P. L. Travers;
with drawings by Mary Shepard.
p. cm.
1. Cookery—Juvenile literature. 2. Literary cookbooks—Juvenile literature.
3. Poppins, Mary (Fictitious character)—Juvenile literature.
I. Shepard, Mary, 1909–2000 II. Title.
TX652.5.T72 2006
641.5'123—dc22   2005031504
ISBN-13: 978-0-15-206080-0 ISBN-10: 0-15-206080-4

A C E G H F D B

Manufactured in China

The type was set in Filosofia.
Illustrations hand tinted by Judythe Sieck
Color separations by Bright Arts Ltd., Hong Kong
Manufactured by South China Printing Company, Ltd., China
This book was printed on totally chlorine-free
80 gsm Ensolux Cream woodfree paper.
Production supervision by Pascha Gerlinger
Designed by April Ward

Mary Poppins

in the Kitchen

I t was Sunday.

All the houses in Cherry-Tree Lane were dozing in the afternoon sun—all except Number Seventeen, which was wide awake with noise and laughter. Mr. and Mrs. Banks were having tea in the nursery with Jane, Michael, John, Barbara, and Annabel.

Suddenly the door opened and in came Mrs. Brill, the cook, with a fresh pot of tea in her hands.

"If you please, ma'am," she said as she set it down. "I have a piece of news." And she pulled a telegram out of her pocket.

"Nothing bad, I hope!" said Mrs. Banks. The very word *news* had an ominous sound, and she eyed the telegram with distrust.

"It's my niece, you see," said Mrs. Brill. "Her four children have all got measles. So I must go and help her."

"Oh, *no!*" cried Mrs. Banks with a shriek. "Why must everything happen at once? Ellen's away nursing a cold, and Mr. Banks and I are on the verge of going to Brighton for a week. George, did you hear?" She turned to her husband. "Mrs. Brill has to go away. What on Earth are we going to do? Who will do the cooking?"

Mr. Banks, down on all fours, pretending to be an elephant with John and Barbara on his back, rose, panting, to his feet.

"Ask Mary Poppins," he replied. "She will manage something."

"But can she cook?" wailed Mrs. Banks. "Breakfasts and suppers would not be hard, but what about the dinners?"

"Humph!" said the well-known voice from the doorway. And the humph was followed by a sniff.

"Of course she can cook," said Mr. Banks. "Mary Poppins can do everything, can't you, Mary Poppins?" Mr. Banks was a tactful man.

Mary Poppins tossed her head. "I have only one pair of hands," she said. "And those are occupied." She had lifted Annabel from the floor, and John and Barbara, one on either side of her, were each hugging a leg.

"I'll lend you mine, Mary Poppins," said Jane. "Then you can have two pairs."

"And mine," said Michael. "I will help you. I'd like to learn to cook."

"Me, too," said John.

"Me, too," said Barbara.

"Could you possibly manage, Mary Poppins? The cab will be here any minute. Perhaps we should cancel it—dear, oh, dear!"

"And when," said Mary Poppins grandly, "have I failed to give satisfaction?"

"Oh, never, never!" cried Mrs. Banks. "I only thought—so much to do—and Robertson Ay so often asleep—and nobody to help you."

Mary Poppins smiled a superior smile. "I have friends and relatives," she said. "And also a cookery book."

"Oh, well, if you really think you can—" Mrs. Banks, relieved and flustered, pushed back her chair and rose. "I'll go and lock my suitcase."

"So that's all right," said Mr. Banks. "We can leave it to Mary Poppins." He poured out another cup of tea, drank it hastily, and went downstairs.

In no time the cab had come to the door, waited while the good-byes were said, and then had rolled away down the lane and disappeared from view.

Mrs. Brill, bag in hand, paused at the front door on her way out.

"I've left you sandwiches for supper and very plain cake."

"Thank you kindly," said Mary Poppins.

"But I thought *we* were going to do the cooking!" said Michael, disappointed.

"There's no cooking in sandwiches, Michael. Tomorrow we will start."

"But you're always telling us, Mary Poppins, that tomorrow never comes."

"Well, call it Monday," said Mary Poppins. "For Monday never fails to come. Now, spit-spot and up the stairs and no more argument."

Jane looked at Michael.

Michael looked at Jane.

"Tomorrow!" they whispered to each other, both feeling that they were on the brink of a new kind of adventure. . . .

 MONDAY

"And a bottle of vanilla essence." Mary Poppins folded her list and put it into her handbag.

The Grocer and his assistants parceled up the great pile of groceries and put them into the perambulator.

"Now, home!" said Mary Poppins briskly as she pushed the perambulator before her and sped along Cherry-Tree Lane and up the garden path. The four children straggled after her, laden with provisions. It had been a busy morning, and they all felt that it was a long time since they had had breakfast.

"What are we cooking today, Mary Poppins?" Jane wanted to know.

"Roast beef," said Mary Poppins. "And Yorkshire pudding to go with it and just a suspicion of cabbage."

"What! No other pudding?" demanded Michael. "I need to end with something sweet."

"Why not gingerbread stars?" said a voice behind them.

They all turned. And there, at the gate of Number Seventeen, were Mrs. Corry, tiny and neat, and her two large daughters, Fannie and Annie.

"We've come to give you a helping hand," said Mrs. Corry gaily.

"But *we're* helping her!" said Michael stoutly.

"Then we will help *you*," said Mrs. Corry as she quickly broke off one of her fingers and gave him a barley-sugar stick.

Fannie and Annie shook hands with all and took the parcels from them.

And in no time they were in the kitchen, eating barley-sugar broken from Mrs. Corry's fingers and getting ready to cook the dinner.

"Where shall we begin?" said Jane.

"At the beginning," said Mary Poppins. "First of all you wash your hands, and then you remember three useful things. Always let *me* switch on the stove, keep away from steaming kettles, and never use the sharper knives unless I am standing by."

"Yes, Mary Poppins," they said gravely. And then they were set to work.

Jane floured and salted the beef, which was put into a hot oven. Michael helped Fannie mix the batter for the Yorkshire pudding, and Annie chopped the cabbage. John and Barbara picked up the scraps and put them into the garbage pail. Annabel, safe in her high chair, sucked at her barley-sugar.

Mary Poppins and Mrs. Corry, each with a cup of tea before her, watched over the whole proceeding.

"And now," said Mrs. Corry, rising, "the first course is safely on its way, so let us get on with the second. Jane and Michael, I have often made gingerbread for you. Now you can make it for me." And she rolled up the sleeves of her little black coat, turned back her skirt till it looked like an apron, and set them both to work.

Michael mixed the flour with the soda and spice and added the ginger and raisins. Jane melted the butter with the sugar and added the egg and the treacle.

"Now put both mixtures into a large bowl and together you can stir."

Mrs. Corry stood over them, carefully watching every movement with her little beady eyes. "It's an excellent recipe," she said. "I had it from King Alfred the Great. He burnt his other cakes, you know, but never his gingerbread."

Jane and Michael scooped the mixture into greased star-shaped tins, and Mrs. Corry put the tins on a tray and popped it into the baking oven.

"There!" she said. "Now, all we need is some golden stars, and I happen to have some with me." And she proceeded to fish from an inner pocket a handful of paper stars.

"You'll save them, won't you?" she asked the children, with an eager look in her eyes.

"Of course we will," said Jane and Michael, for they knew from old experience that Mrs. Corry's golden stars had a special kind of magic. Some night, if they looked from the nursery window, they would see her perched on a tall ladder, pasting the stars on the sky, with the help of Mary Poppins.

Now there was nothing to do but wait, to baste the roast from time to time, to put the Yorkshire pudding into the oven for the last half hour, and to add sugar and salt to the cabbage to help it to keep its flavour.

"Ten minutes at the most in boiling water. Cabbage needs to be crisp," said Mary Poppins.

And then, at last, she called out, "Ready!" and they all sat round the kitchen table, eating a meal fit for a prince, keeping a plateful for Robertson Ay, who was sleeping in the china cupboard.

"What a beautiful cook I am!" said Michael as he helped himself to a gingerbread star.

Mary Poppins gave a sniff. "Handsome is as handsome does," she said with an uppish smile as she led the Corrys to the front door and said a polite good-bye.

 TUESDAY

"What is the plan for today, Mary Poppins?" asked Jane as she and Michael dried the breakfast dishes.

"She's planning to go to sea, of course!" said a voice outside the open kitchen window. And there in the garden stood Admiral Boom, with his Admiral's hat on the back of his head and his telescope under his arm.

Jane and Michael threw down their cloths and ran to open the kitchen door.

"Yo, ho, ho and a bottle of rum!" they cried, pulling the Admiral into the kitchen and hugging him round the waist.

"Ahoy there, my hearties! Hoist the mainsail! Well, Mary Poppins, all alone? What are you having for dinner today?"

"Well, yesterday it was roast beef. So today it has to be shepherd's pie."

"Of course it does," said Admiral Boom. "Shepherd's pie always comes after roast beef. It uses up the remains. Well, pipe the Admiral aboard and he'll help you in the galley. What about vegetables?" he said as he plucked Mrs. Brill's apron from behind the door and tied it round his waist.

"Carrots," said Mary Poppins briskly. "And mashed potatoes for the top of the pie and apple charlotte to follow."

"Good!" said the Admiral. "Now, all hands on deck. Ship's company, quick march!"

The children rushed to do his bidding. Michael brought him the mincing machine. Jane brought the cold roast beef from the icebox. John and Barbara gave him the chopping board.

"There we are, that's all shipshape. We'll screw the machine to the edge of the table and chop up the meat and put it in.

> 'Follow the fleet and fly with me,
> Far away to the foaming sea,'"

sang Admiral Boom as he turned the handle.

Then Jane and Michael took a hand at the turning, and very soon the cold roast beef became a plateful of minced meat. Jane spooned it into a baking dish while Michael, watched over by the Admiral, sprinkled it with pepper and salt.

"Ropes and rigging, cockles and shrimps! Now, all we need is a chopped onion—" The Admiral darted to the vegetable basket. "And a spoonful or two of chopped parsley and some leftover gravy." He opened the door of the kitchen cupboard. "And once we've cooked and mashed the potatoes, we'll spread them all over the top, and in with it to the oven. Belay there! Now for the apple charlotte! Blast my gizzard, Mary Poppins, you're doing all the work yourself!"

"A stitch in time saves nine," said Mary Poppins primly as she finished the scraping of the carrots and turned to peel the apples. "Now, one of you can butter a pie dish and put in the apples in layers. Another can sprinkle them with sugar, and a third can cover them with bread crumbs. Apple charlotte," she warned them all, "should be soft and sticky and moist and rich."

"Ay, ay, it's just the dish for a sailor. Heave to and let down the anchor, messmates. If Mary Poppins says, 'Stay to dinner,' I won't go to sea after all."

Of course Mary Poppins could not refuse, and the Admiral delighted them all by having two helpings of shepherd's pie and three of apple charlotte.

And nobody noticed, least of all Admiral Boom, that when at last he took his leave, he still had Mrs. Brill's apron tied firmly round his waist.

# WEDNESDAY

"There now!" said Mary Poppins as she settled Annabel into the perambulator and wheeled it into the garden.

"And now to work," she ordered the children as she led them all into the kitchen.

At that moment the doorbell rang, and presently Robertson Ay came in, yawning and looking sleepy.

"You've got visitors," he said wearily. "By the name of Mr. and Mrs. Turvy."

He ushered two people into the room and collapsed upon a chair in the doorway.

"Why, Cousin Arthur, what a surprise! And you, too, Topsy!" cried Mary Poppins.

Jane and Michael ran to greet the curious-looking guests, both of whom were wearing their clothes back to front.

"But this is Wednesday," said Michael. "I thought that only happened on Tuesdays." He gazed at Mr. Turvy's jacket, which was buttoned down the back, and at Mrs. Turvy's straw hat with its feather facing forward.

"It's all altered," said Mr. Turvy. "It happens every day now. We're topsy-turvier than ever. But still we thought we'd come and help."

"A very kind thought," said Mary Poppins. "We're having Irish stew today and then honey and bananas."

"Better have upside-down cake. More suitable," said Mr. Turvy.

So everybody set to work. And though the guests behaved in a topsy-turvy manner—Mrs. Turvy repeatedly stood on her head and Mr. Turvy insisted on looking for the lamb chops in the broom cupboard—the cooking got under way.

Under Mary Poppins' watchful eye the children peeled potatoes and onions and put them in the casserole. Michael added the lamb chops. Jane covered it all with water, and Mr. Turvy was politely prevented from adding a touch of sugar.

"Irish stew cooks itself," said Mary Poppins as she put the casserole into the oven. "So we can concentrate on the cake. Michael, you may slice the peaches, and Jane can make the batter. No, Topsy, the egg must be beaten to a froth; it does not have to be fried!"

Jane stirred and stirred with a wooden spoon till the butter was creamed and the sugar added. And, gradually, in spite of Mr. Turvy's efforts to add some unnecessary salt and Mrs. Turvy's powdering her nose with sifted flour, the ingredients were mixed together, the batter poured over the sliced peaches, and the cake put in the oven.

"Now, all we have to do is wait," said Mary Poppins calmly. "Won't you sit down?" she asked the Turvys.

"I'd like to sit down," said Mr. Turvy, "but, of course, as everything's back to front, I cannot help standing up."

"Why don't we dance?" said Mrs. Turvy. "That's better than sitting down." And she began to turn, feet over head, round and round

the kitchen table. Mr. Turvy sighed but followed, and their topsy-turvy behaviour was so infectious that presently everyone was dancing, or turning head over heels. Jane and Michael pranced and polkaed, John and Barbara skipped and spun. Even Mary Poppins, holding out the strings of her apron, waltzed primly round the table. The only people not dancing were Annabel, who was scraping out the batter bowl, and Robertson Ay, who was sound asleep.

"Enough!" said Mary Poppins at last. "Everything must be cooked by now."

Her word was enough. The whirling kitchen steadied itself. Everyone came to a halt. Michael carefully took the stew from the oven. Jane turned the cake out downside up and covered it with whipped cream.

"It's a great success!" said Mary Poppins. "We won't call it upside-down cake ever again. Its name will be Topsy-Turvy!"

THURSDAY

"That's one thing done!" said Mary Poppins as she swept the dust into a pan and put the broom away. She glanced round the spotless kitchen floor and seemed to be pleased with her handiwork.

"Mary Poppins," said Michael as he watched her tie on a fresh white apron. "Who do you think will come today?"

"Why should anyone come, may I ask?"

"To help us," said Jane, "to cook the dinner."

"We don't need help," said Mary Poppins. "It's a very simple meal today—beef patties with green peas and bread-and-butter pudding."

"That sounds delicious! May I come in?"

At these words everybody turned. And there stood a small chubby old man in a frock coat and baggy trousers and a long white beard down to his waist.

"Cousin Fred!" exclaimed Mary Poppins.

"Mr. Twigley!" the children cried.

"The front door was open, Mary, my dear, and a young man was sleeping on the doormat. So I just stepped over him and came in."

"Will you get any wishes today?" asked Michael.

"Oh, dear me, no! They only happen on the first New Moon after the Second Wet Sunday after the Third of May. I can't just *wish* the

patties cooked. But I'll help wherever I can." Mr. Twigley took up a fork, ran his fingers lightly across it, and a stave of music sounded.

"Now, Fred, we do need something more than music!"

"Of course you do, Mary, my dear." Mr. Twigley put a spoon to his lips and blew a flute-like phrase. "You must shape the meat into neat round cakes, press them lightly with the hands, and fry them in a dry pan or put them under the grill." He sang the words in a shaky tenor voice.

"I'll do it," sang Michael, imitating Mr. Twigley. "Give me the meat."

"Jane," warbled Mary Poppins sweetly, "you must put the slices of buttered bread in layers into a buttered pie dish."

"And sprinkle raisins between the layers and cover it all with a simple custard," trilled Jane in a high soprano.

"Me, too! Me, too!" chanted John and Barbara in their shrill small voices.

And there they all were, singing and cooking, with Mr. Twigley making music with everything he touched. He struck two saucepan lids together and made them sound like cymbals. He took the egg whisk and plucked the wire, and there was a small guitar. He thumped on the pie dish with his fists till it gave forth a roll of drums. He made knives sound like violins and soup spoons like xylophones. And when the beef patties were ready and the pudding came brown and crisp from the oven, they arrived together on the table with a lordly blare of a trumpet blown through a stalk of celery.

"Splendid!" said Mr. Twigley proudly, as though he had cooked the whole meal himself. "And I find that I do have a wish after all!"

"But will it come true?" demanded Jane.

"It depends on her," said Mr. Twigley, nodding at Mary Poppins. "I do so wish, Mary, my dear, that we could make a picnic of it and take our meal into the garden."

"Oh, please, Mary Poppins!" cried Jane and Michael.

But Mary Poppins, as if by magic, was already out under the elm tree and spreading a tablecloth in its shade.

"That was a wonderful wish," said Jane as they all sat around the tablecloth eating beef patties and peas.

Mr. Twigley plucked a blade of grass and ran it lightly over his lips till it sounded like an English horn.

"Mr. Twigley," demanded Michael. "Has everything got its own true music?"

"Everything," answered Mr. Twigley.

"And everybody?" Jane inquired.

"Everybody," he said.

# FRIDAY

Jane was sitting by the kitchen window, waiting to hear the menu for the day.

"There's a pigeon," she said, "staring in at me. What can it want? Oh, it's flown away."

"Well, let it fly," said Mary Poppins. "I've quite enough birds to think of, thank you, with roast chicken and bread sauce for dinner and green beans and fruit salad."

"Feed the birds, tuppence a bag!" A familiar voice sounded outside in the garden.

"It's the Bird Woman!" cried the children together as Michael ran to the kitchen door.

And there, indeed, the Bird Woman stood, with a ring of pigeons about her. In one hand she carried her basket of bread crumbs and in the other a bunch of herbs.

"My birdie told me you were at home, so I thought I'd drop in to have a little chat and to see how you were faring."

"Mustn't grumble," said Mary Poppins. "We're doing nicely, thank you."

"And chicken for dinner, my dears, I see. So these will come in handy."

The Bird Woman waved her bunch of herbs and handed them to Michael.

"Tuck them inside him, love," she said. "They'll make him sweet and tasty."

So the chicken was stuffed full of garden herbs, rubbed with salt and lemon juice, and popped inside the oven. The green beans were washed and stripped. And the Bird Woman's pigeons flew round the kitchen, perching on shelves or the backs of chairs and sometimes on the children's shoulders.

"And now the bread sauce," said Mary Poppins. "You take the bread, Jane, and crumble it—"

"Wait a minute!" the Bird Woman cried. And she opened several bagfuls of crumbs and poured them into a saucepan.

"That will save you some work, my chick. Now all we need is milk and butter and a small onion for flavour."

The Bird Woman stood by the kitchen stove, stirring the sauce with a wooden spoon. She salted it and peppered it. And her birds clustered close about her, one on her hat and another in her pocket.

"Now we'll set it aside and warm it when the chicken's ready. It will be a sauce fit for a king. Well, I must be off."

"But you'll stay to dinner, ma'am, surely?" Mary Poppins, her hands full of bananas, oranges, apples, and pears, made a gesture of invitation. "Jane and Michael are going to make a fruit salad."

"No, no. I must be on my way. My other birdies are waiting. You've got your birds to feed. I've got mine."

The Bird Woman, under a cloud of wings, straightened her hat and took up her basket.

"I'll take you to the gate," said Michael. And he and Jane and John and Barbara followed her down the path.

"Feed the birds!" the Bird Woman cried as she stepped out into the lane. "Tuppence a bag! Feed the birds!"

"We'll see you at St. Paul's," called the children as they watched her hurrying down the lane, looking like a mother hen amid a flock of chickens.

# SATURDAY

Jane and Michael ran into the kitchen, with Andrew and Willoughby, Miss Lark's dogs, yapping breathlessly at their heels.

"We found them out in the lane," said Michael, "so we brought them home with us. What are we cooking today, Mary Poppins?"

"Lancashire hot pot and cherry pie. You can get the hot pot ready, and Jane can make the pastry."

There was an air of quiet busyness about the kitchen as they all prepared the dinner. Michael put alternate layers of meat, potatoes, and onion into a casserole. Jane worked shortening and flour together to make pastry for the pie. John and Barbara pulled the stems off the cherries and put the fruit into a pie dish. And the dogs looked on with interest.

"Mary Poppins, where are you? Help, oh, help!" A wild cry shattered the peaceful scene. And there in the doorway stood Miss Lark with the Park Keeper behind her.

"Oh, Mary Poppins, I've lost the dogs. They're not in my garden, not in the lane, and the Park Keeper has searched all over the Park."

"They're here," said Mary Poppins calmly as the dogs rose lazily to their feet and sauntered toward Miss Lark.

"Oh dear, oh dear, what a relief! I thought I should have to inform the police. Even, perhaps, the Prime Minister. Andrew and Willoughby, you ran away! How could you be so heartless?"

31

"Observe the rules!" the Park Keeper cried from the door. "All litter to be placed in the baskets."

Mary Poppins eyed him sternly.

"We are observing the rules, thank you. And we've got no litter here."

"I shall put you both on the lead," said Miss Lark as she stooped toward the dogs' collars. "And take you home at once. There now, you shan't escape again. Thank you for keeping them, Mary Poppins. They might have been lost to me forever. Well, I must be going. Thank you, thank you! I see you are all extremely busy. What clever children—making pastry! When will Mrs. Banks be back? Tomorrow? Splendid! Come, dogs! Good-bye!"

And away went Miss Lark, in her usual bustle, with the dogs behind her looking sheepish and glancing back longingly at the children.

The Park Keeper sighed a wistful sigh as he eyed the laden table.

"Cooking?" he inquired with interest.

"What else does one do in a kitchen?" Mary Poppins gave him a mocking glance.

"I could stay and give you a helping hand, supposing you wanted it," he said.

"And supposing I didn't?" she said calmly as she edged him out of the kitchen.

"It's me dinner hour," said the Park Keeper, eagerly sniffing the air.

Mary Poppins was not to be cajoled.

"Then you'd better go and get something to eat," she told him scornfully.

The Park Keeper made a last effort as she thrust him from the house.

"I'm partial to hot pot and cherry pie." He made a pleading gesture.

"So am I," said Mary Poppins. And she closed the door upon him.

SUNDAY

"I'm excited," said Michael as he dried the last of the lettuce leaves, wrapped them in a fresh napkin, and put them into the icebox. "What time will they arrive, Mary Poppins?"

"The letter said at one o'clock. And good cooks are never excited, Michael. It spoils what they are cooking."

Mary Poppins broke an egg in two, quickly divided the white from the yolk, and put each into a separate bowl. This she did four times. Then she turned the bowl of whites over to Jane and handed her the eggbeater. "Beat them until they're stiff," she said.

Outside in the lane, the Policeman was walking up and down, hoping, perhaps, for a glimpse of Ellen. And the Ice Cream Man wheeled his tricycle past, ringing his bell to attract attention.

But away in the kitchen nobody noticed. They were all of them far too busy.

"Now, Michael," said Mary Poppins briskly. "Lightly dip the chicken strips into two beaten eggs and then into the bread crumbs. And you, Jane, measure two ounces of butter and one and a half of flour. John and Barbara will set the table."

Mary Poppins was like a whirlwind, turning from one to another and helping each in turn. And in between times she stood at the stove stirring something in a saucepan, adding this and adding that and tasting the result with a smack of her lips.

The morning wore on, and at last it seemed that all was prepared. It was time to put something under the grill and something else into the oven.

And just at the moment this was done, the kitchen clock struck a single note and a latchkey turned in the front door.

"They're here! They're here!" cried everyone.

The four children streamed out of the kitchen, screaming cries of welcome. And presently they were back again with Mr. and Mrs. Banks, all of them wrapped in one big embrace and everybody laughing.

"Still alive, Mary Poppins?" asked Mr. Banks as he plucked Annabel from her high chair and handed her to her mother.

Mrs. Banks fluttered and cooed and kissed as the children clustered about her.

"I do believe you've grown!" she told them.

"Nonsense, my dear," said Mr. Banks. "We've only been away a week. Mary Poppins, we're hungry," he said, turning. "Do you think you could manage a cheese sandwich or maybe a couple of boiled eggs?"

Mary Poppins and Jane and Michael exchanged a glance full of meaning.

"If you'll take your places in the dining room," said Mary Poppins, "the children will bring you something to eat."

"How good to be home," said Mr. Banks as they settled into their chairs. "I'm looking forward to a little snack. But what is this?" he demanded, turning.

There in the doorway stood the four children, each of them carrying a dish. And behind them, like a pillar of starch, was the figure of Mary Poppins.

"It isn't a snack," said Michael, laughing. "We've cooked you a real dinner." He put down his dish and took off the lid. "Chicken," he said triumphantly, "with potatoes from John and salad from Barbara."

"And a lemon soufflé from me," said Jane as she put her dish on the table.

Mr. Banks stared at Mrs. Banks and Mrs. Banks stared back.

"Salad! Potatoes! Chicken! Soufflé! Can we believe our eyes, my dear?" Mr. Banks was amazed.

"We must be dreaming," said Mrs. Banks as she gazed at the spreading feast. "Can the children have cooked all this? So all has gone well, after all, Mary Poppins?" She smiled her timid smile.

Mary Poppins tossed her head and gave a familiar sniff.

"Of course it has," she said calmly. "What else did you expect?"

Mary Poppins'

Cookery Book

from A to Z

*"All that is or was or will be happens between
A and Z," says Mary Poppins. "And that
includes this cookery book."*

A CAUTION FROM MARY POPPINS

First of all wash your hands, and then remember three useful things: Always let an adult switch on the stove, keep away from steaming kettles, and never use knives unless an adult is standing by.

Apple Charlotte or Apple Brown Betty

2 pounds apples—greenings or Cortlands
½ cup or 1 stick butter
2 cups fresh white bread crumbs
1½ cups dark brown sugar
deep pie dish that will hold at least 1 quart—a soufflé dish will do

Heat the oven to 350°.

Choose apples that are hard and juicy. Peel and core them and slice as thin as you can. Butter the pie dish, using a little of the ½ cup. Sprinkle with bread crumbs. They will stick to the butter and make a comfortable bed for the apples. Lay a thick layer of sliced apples on the bread crumbs and scatter some brown sugar on top. Dot all over with little pieces of butter. Start all over again with a layer of apples, bread crumbs, sugar, and butter and continue the layers until the dish is full. Make the last layer of bread crumbs. Pile it high. The apples shrink as they cook. Cook for 1 hour. Mary Poppins serves this pudding lukewarm with whipped cream.

Beef Patties or Small Hamburgers

1½ pounds lean, minced (ground) sirloin of beef or top round
4 teaspoons Worcestershire sauce
salt and pepper

Divide the ground or minced beef into 6 equal portions. Shape, with your hands, into round patties 3 inches in diameter and 1 inch thick, pressing lightly. Heat a heavy frying pan or skillet over medium heat for 3–4 minutes. Cook patties for 3–4 minutes on one side. Turn over and cook for 3–4 minutes on the other. Three minutes on each side will be rare, and 5 minutes will be well-done patties.

Remove to a serving platter. Pour the Worcestershire sauce into the hot pan. Stir quickly with a wooden spoon and pour over the patties. Season with salt and pepper.

Makes 6 servings.

Bread-and-Butter Pudding

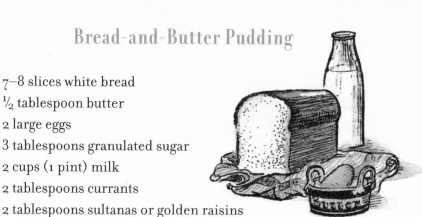

7–8 slices white bread

½ tablespoon butter

2 large eggs

3 tablespoons granulated sugar

2 cups (1 pint) milk

2 tablespoons currants

2 tablespoons sultanas or golden raisins

1-quart soufflé or pie dish

Heat the oven to 350°.

Remove the crusts from the bread and, with Mary Poppins at your side, cut each slice in half lengthwise, making 14–16 very thin slices. Butter them on one side.

Beat the eggs and sugar together in a bowl. Add the milk and beat again. With a little butter, grease the inside of the dish. Lay two slices on the bottom, butter side up, and sprinkle with a quarter of the raisins and currants. Lay two more slices of buttered bread on top, buttered side up, and sprinkle with currants and raisins. Continue till there are only 4 slices left. Sprinkle remaining currants and raisins on top. Fit 2 slices into each side of the dish between the side and the layered bread. Fold them over so that they make a sort of lid. Pour the eggs and milk into the dish and wait for half an hour before baking in the middle of the preheated oven.

Bake for 40 minutes, at which time the top will be brown and crisp.

Cherry Pie

2 pounds cherries

sugar

1 cup water

1 egg yolk

deep pie dish that holds 1 quart

Pastry: Make the same amount as specified for jam tarts,
   on page 53, and use the same recipe.

Wash the cherries. Remove the stems and the stones (pits).
Make a layer of cherries about 1 inch thick in the pie dish. Sprinkle
lightly with sugar. The amount to use depends on whether the cherries are sweet or sour. Make a second layer and sprinkle with sugar.
Continue in this way till the dish is full. Pile them up in the dish so
that there is a nice dome of fruit. Add 1 cup of water.

Heat the oven to 350°.

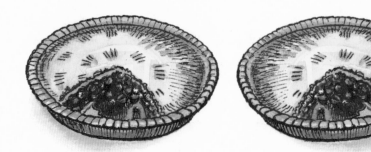

Prepare the pastry: Mix the egg yolk with 1 tablespoon of water. Roll out the pastry. It should be about ¼ inch thick. Roll it onto the rolling pin. Brush the edge of the pie dish with the egg and water mixture. This is called a glaze. Roll the pastry off the rolling pin and onto the pie dish, covering it completely. Trim it evenly with a small knife, saving the bits. Press gently to the rim of the dish to seal it. Gather the bits and form a ball. Roll it out again. Brush the entire surface of the covered pie. Cut long strips, about ½ inch wide, and fit them neatly round the edge of the dish, pressing them into place. Mark them evenly with the tines of a fork. Make pretty cutouts with the rest of the pastry—leaves and flowers or your initials—and place them on the pie top. Brush the surface again with the glaze.

Bake in the middle of the oven for 30 minutes. When you take it out of the oven, sprinkle with some sugar while it's still hot.

Date Bread

1¾ cups sifted all-purpose flour (sift first and then measure)
½ teaspoon salt
¼ teaspoon cream of tartar
¾ teaspoon baking soda
⅓ cup softened butter
⅔ cup granulated sugar
1 egg
1 cup chopped dates
loaf pan, 7½ inches x 3¼ inches x 2¼ inches

Heat the oven to 350°.

Butter the inside of the pan lightly.

Sift the measured flour, salt, cream of tartar, and soda into a small bowl. In a mixing bowl, cream the butter and sugar together till light and fluffy. If you don't have a mixer, use a large wooden spoon. Beat the egg thoroughly and mix with the butter and sugar. It will look curdled. Don't worry—that's how it should be. Stir in the flour, bit by bit, till thoroughly mixed. Then stir in the chopped dates. Mix again. The dough will be very thick and heavy. Spoon into the buttered loaf pan.

Bake for 1 hour in the middle of the oven. Turn out on a wire rack to cool.

Dressing for Salads

1 teaspoon sugar

½ teaspoon salt

¼ teaspoon dry mustard

3 tablespoons oil (olive or your favourite vegetable oil)

1 tablespoon red wine vinegar

Mix the ingredients in a small glass jar with a screw top.

Shake thoroughly before pouring over your salad and tossing. If this mixture is too sweet, reduce the amount of sugar.

"There are some," says Mary Poppins, "who like it without any sugar."

Easter Cake

6 large eggs

1 cup sugar

½ teaspoon almond extract

1 cup sifted all-purpose flour (sift first and then measure)

6 tablespoons melted butter

9-inch ring mold or tube pan

Heat the oven to 350°.

Butter lightly the mold or pan and dust with flour.

Choose a large bowl that will fit over a saucepan of very hot, but not boiling, water. Break the eggs into the bowl and start beating right away. Beat for about 5 minutes, by which time the eggs will be light and fluffy and pale yellow. Add the sugar gradually and continue beating. This is hard work and will take 15–20 minutes. If you have an electric beater, so much the better. Add the almond extract and beat till the eggs have almost tripled in volume. When you lift the beater, the mixture should stand in peaks. Fold in the flour very gently and thoroughly, and lastly the melted butter, very gently. Spoon the mixture carefully into the prepared pan and bake on the middle shelf of the oven for 35 minutes.

Take it out of the oven and turn it upside down on a wire rack to cool. If it does not drop out of the pan of its own accord after 7 or 8 minutes, help it by running a knife around the edge and giving it a few gentle taps.

Fruit Salad

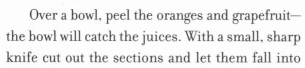

2 oranges
1 grapefruit
1 apple
1 pear
$\frac{1}{4}$ pound grapes
1 banana
1 pint strawberries (optional)

Over a bowl, peel the oranges and grapefruit—
the bowl will catch the juices. With a small, sharp
knife cut out the sections and let them fall into
the bowl. Squeeze the juice out of what is left. Peel and core the apple
and pear. Slice or dice—whichever shape you prefer, but not both.
Mix with the oranges and grapefruit. The citrus will prevent the
apple and pear from turning brown.

Wash the grapes, and if they are not seedless, cut them in half
and remove the seeds.

Peel and slice the banana. Mix with the other fruits.

If the salad is not sweet enough, stir in some fine sugar. There
will be enough natural juices without adding a syrup.

Lastly and just before serving, wash and hull the strawberries.
Cut them in half and mix with the other fruits.

Mary Poppins serves this with whipped cream for special
parties.

Gingerbread Stars

$3/4$ cup all-purpose flour

$1/2$ teaspoon baking soda

$1/2$ teaspoon mixed spices—nutmeg, cloves, and cinnamon

1 teaspoon powdered ginger

$1/4$ cup seedless raisins

$1/4$ cup or 4 tablespoons butter

$1/2$ cup, packed full, dark brown sugar

2 tablespoons dark molasses (dark treacle)

1 egg, well beaten

baking sheet lightly buttered and dusted with flour

2 6-inch star shapes, buttered and floured,
  or 1 8-inch sandwich cake pan

Heat the oven to 350°.

Sift into a mixing bowl the flour, soda, spices, and ginger. Stir in the raisins. Melt the butter and sugar together in a small saucepan over low heat. Remove from the stove and allow to cool a little. Add the molasses and then stir with the beaten egg into the spiced flour and mix well with a large wooden spoon. Place the two star shapes on the buttered baking sheet. Divide the batter equally between the two star shapes or fill the sandwich cake tin.

Bake the stars for 30 minutes and the cake tin for 40 minutes in the middle of the oven. "If you don't have star-shaped tins, use a round one, eight inches in diameter, and then you have 'full moons,'" says Mary Poppins.

Turn out on a wire rack to cool.

Honey and Bananas

2 tablespoons butter

3 bananas, not too ripe

¹/₄ cup honey

¹/₄ cup water

2 tablespoons lemon juice

ovenproof dish, approximately 9 inches x 15 inches

Heat the oven to 350°.

Grease the dish with a little of the butter.

Peel the bananas and cut in half lengthwise. Fit them into the buttered dish. Mix the honey, water, and lemon juice together and pour over the bananas. Dot with what's left of the butter.

Bake for 30 minutes. Baste with the juices frequently. When the bananas are done, there should be little liquid in the dish, and it will be like a thick syrup.

Irish Stew

4 pounds lamb shoulder chops
3 pounds potatoes (the old crop is best)
3 large onions
salt and freshly ground black pepper
3- or 4-quart casserole with lid

Heat the oven to 325°.

Ask the butcher to cup up the chops. Pieces about 2 inches square are good. Remove all fat. Peel and slice the potatoes. They should be as thick as 2 quarters. Peel the onions and slice them as thin as possible. Cover the bottom of the casserole with a layer of potatoes, then a layer of the lamb pieces, followed by sliced onion. Sprinkle with salt and freshly ground black pepper. Begin all over again with layers of potato, lamb, and onion, sprinkled with salt and pepper. Continue until all the lamb is used up. End with a layer of potatoes. Pour in enough cold water to reach the level of the top layer of potatoes.

Cook for 2 hours, covered, in the oven. Cool and skim off fat, if any.

Heat again in the oven before serving. Half an hour should be enough at 350°. There will be ample for 6 or 8 servings.

Jam Tarts

The Pastry:

2 cups sifted all-purpose flour

½ teaspoon salt

3 tablespoons vegetable shortening

8 tablespoons or 1 stick cold butter

iced water

Heat the oven to 400°.

Sift the flour and salt into a mixing bowl. Add the shortening, and chip the cold butter into the bowl. Break up with a pastry blender until the mixture is coarse and mealy. Add enough cold water to form a ball (about 3 tablespoons), handling as little as possible.

Transfer the dough to a floured board. Spread out with the heel of your hand once, gather into a ball, and seal in a plastic bag or plastic wrap. Place in the refrigerator for at least 2 hours.

Roll out the dough. It should be between ⅛ inch and ¼ inch thick. Fit it into small tart tins. It is best first to cut pieces roughly the size of the tins and, after they have been pressed firmly into each tin, trim the edges neatly with a sharp knife. Prick the pastry all over with a fork. This allows the air, trapped between the pan and the pastry, to escape and prevents the pastry from rising.

Put all the tart tins on a baking sheet and bake in the middle of the oven for 10–12 minutes. Take them out of the oven and fill with jam while they are still hot.

Kale (Cabbage)

3 pounds kale
3 quarts water
3 tablespoons salt
2 tablespoons butter
salt and freshly ground black pepper

Wash the kale in running water. Cut out the coarse stalks. In a large pot bring the water to a boil. Add the salt. Throw in the kale leaves and boil rapidly, without a lid, for 4–5 minutes or until the leaves are tender. Drain very well in a colander and press out any water that is left.

Melt the butter in a smaller pan. Chop the kale and mix with the butter till hot. Add salt and freshly ground black pepper.

Kings' or Twelfth Night Cake

1 cup (½ pound) softened butter

1 cup granulated sugar

4 eggs

2 tablespoons milk

3 cups self-rising flour

1 dried bean

cake tin, 8 inches round x 3 inches deep, lightly greased
    with butter and dusted with flour

Heat the oven to 325°.

Cream the butter and sugar together till light and fluffy. Beat the eggs and the milk and add gradually to the butter and sugar. Continue beating while adding the flour.

Spoon into prepared cake tin. Drop the bean into the batter. Bake for 1¼ hours. Cool on a wire rack.

"Everyone knows," says Mary Poppins, "that the bean is there for a purpose. Whoever finds it in his piece of cake is sure to have great good luck."

Lancashire Hot Pot

2 pounds best end of neck of lamb (neck or shoulder chops)
3 lamb kidneys
salt and freshly ground black pepper
2 pounds potatoes
3 onions, small to medium
1 pinch of dried thyme or 2–3 sprigs of fresh
1 small bay leaf
½ cup beef stock
2 tablespoons melted butter
3- or 4-quart casserole with a lid

Heat the oven to 350°.

Ask the butcher to cut the chops into bite-size pieces. Remove all the fat. The meat may be removed from the bone, but Mary Poppins prefers not to because, left on, it gives a good flavour to the hot pot.

Skin and cut the kidneys in half and in half again. Cut out the center fatty core. Season the meats generously with salt, freshly ground black pepper, and the crumbled bay leaf. Peel the potatoes and slice them rather thickly, about ⅜ of an inch. Peel and chop the onions finely. Butter the inside of a casserole. Cover the bottom with a layer of potato slices. Sprinkle with a little thyme. Stand the cut-up chops upright on the layer of potatoes with a piece of kidney between each one. Sprinkle with chopped onion and cover with a layer of potatoes and then lamb and kidney. Continue in this way till all have been used up, ending with a layer of potatoes. Pour in enough beef stock to come up to the bottom of the top layer of potatoes. Brush potatoes with melted butter. Cover with a lid and bake for 1 hour.

Lemon Soufflé

4 tablespoons or ½ stick butter
4 tablespoons all-purpose flour
1 cup warm milk
1 large lemon, grated and squeezed
4 tablespoons granulated sugar
3 egg yolks
4 egg whites
pinch of cream of tartar
pinch of salt
1-quart soufflé dish
baking sheet

Heat the oven to 400°.

Butter the inside of the soufflé dish. Sprinkle with granulated sugar. Turn it upside down to remove the surplus.

In a heavy saucepan melt the butter till it foams. Turn down the flame and stir in the flour. Cook for 2–3 minutes. Stir all the time to prevent the flour from scorching. This mixture is called a roux. Take the pan off the fire and pour in the milk all at once. Stir vigorously and return to gentle heat. Stir till the sauce thickens. Add lemon rind. Stir in the sugar and remove pan from the fire again. Turn off the heat. It won't be needed again. Allow the mixture to cool.

Separate 3 eggs. Stir in the yolks and the lemon juice. This mixture is now called the soufflé base. Separate one more egg and add the white to the others in the bowl. Now you have 4 egg whites. Beat till they foam and froth. Add a pinch of cream of tartar and a pinch of salt. Continue beating till stiff peaks remain when the beater or whisk is removed.

Using a large metal spoon, stir 1 heaped spoonful of egg whites into the soufflé base. Spoon this mixture into the bowl containing the egg whites. Fold one mixture into the other until all the whites have been evenly mixed with the base. Don't overdo it or you will burst the small egg-white bubbles. Spoon carefully into the prepared soufflé dish.

Put the dish on a baking sheet for easy lifting in and out of the oven. Bake for 15 minutes. Sprinkle the top with fine sugar and serve immediately. You must wait for the soufflé—it won't wait for you.

Meringues

3 egg whites
pinch of salt
pinch of cream of tartar
$^3/_4$ cup granulated sugar
2 baking or cookie sheets

Set the oven at 250°.

Lightly grease the baking or cookie sheets with butter. Dust with flour and shake to remove the surplus.

Beat the egg whites with a whisk or rotary beater till frothy. Add salt and cream of tartar. Continue beating until mixture holds shape. Gradually add the sugar and continue till mixture is very stiff and shining. Long, hard beating is very necessary. Drop the mixture onto the prepared baking sheets by the tablespoonful.

Bake for 45–50 minutes until meringues are firm to the touch. Turn off the oven and leave the door open. After 1 hour remove the meringues with a spatula.

Mary Poppins sandwiches two together with sweetened whipped cream for a special treat.

Nut Loaf

2 cups all-purpose sifted flour
4 teaspoons baking powder
½ cup granulated sugar
1 teaspoon salt
⅓ cup butter
1 egg, well beaten
1 cup cold milk
1 cup shelled nuts, finely chopped (walnuts, pecans, or hazels)
loaf pan, 8½ inches x 4½ inches x 2½ inches, buttered
and floured

Heat the oven to 350°.

Sift the flour and baking powder together into a mixing bowl. Add the sugar and salt. Cut the butter into small pieces and rub into the flour with your fingertips or a pastry cutter. It should now look and feel like coarse cornmeal. Beat the egg and milk together and add gradually to the flour and butter mixture, beating very hard. Stir in chopped nuts. Turn into prepared loaf pan.

Wait 20 minutes before baking. Bake in middle of the oven for 1 hour.

Turn out on wire rack. Cool before cutting.

Oatmeal Cookies

2 eggs

1 cup granulated sugar

1 pinch of salt

2 cups quick oats

baking or cookie sheet greased lightly with butter

Heat the oven to 450°.

In a mixing bowl beat the eggs and sugar together till light in colour and creamy. Stir in the salt and oatmeal. Drop the batter, teaspoonful by teaspoonful, onto the baking sheet about 4 inches apart—they will spread—and flatten with the bottom of a glass dipped in water.

Bake for 5 minutes until the edges are golden. Remove from the sheet with a spatula at once and cool on a wire rack.

"This recipe," says Mary Poppins, "will make about three dozen sweet biscuits or cookies. Very good to store for a rainy day."

Potatoes

Potatoes are a most useful vegetable and may be cooked in many different ways. When they are new and small, they should be scrubbed with a hard brush and cooked in boiling salted water—1 tablespoon to a quart—to which a large sprig of mint has been added. Cook till tender, about 15 minutes, depending on the size. Served with butter, this makes a separate course to a meal.

To bake potatoes, wash but do not peel. Rub the skins lightly with butter or oil and bake for about 45 minutes in a 450° oven. Before serving, make two deep cuts, crosswise, and squeeze the potatoes so that they open. Pop a teaspoon of butter into the gap.

Potatoes cooked in their jackets, peeled, and mashed with a little butter, milk or cream, and salt and pepper are good served with sausages.

Queen of Puddings

1⅔ cups milk

2 tablespoons granulated sugar

2 whole eggs

2 egg yolks

¼ teaspoon vanilla extract

1 cup loosely packed white bread crumbs.

deep pie dish that will hold 1 quart—a soufflé dish will do

a little butter for greasing the dish

The Topping:

2 egg whites

2 tablespoons sugar

2 tablespoons raspberry jam

Heat the oven to 350°.

Heat the milk with the sugar till very hot but not quite boiling. Beat the whole eggs and egg yolks and add vanilla. Stir a little of the beaten egg into the hot milk and then pour all of the milk into the remainder of the egg mixture. Stir thoroughly and mix in bread crumbs. Put in a greased pie or soufflé dish and bake in the middle of the oven for 25 minutes.

Beat the egg whites until there are soft peaks when you lift out the beater. Sprinkle 1 tablespoon of sugar over the egg whites and continue beating. Sprinkle with the remainder of the sugar and beat a little longer.

Take the pie dish out of the oven and dot evenly with raspberry jam. Spoon the beaten egg whites over the top. Mary Poppins likes it best when the surface looks sort of rough. Return to the oven and bake for an additional 20 minutes. Mary Poppins says, "If this pudding is good enough for a queen, it is good enough for grown-ups."

Roast Chicken and Bread Sauce

1 chicken, weighing between 3 and 3½ pounds
salt and pepper
1 large handful fresh parsley
juice of 1 lemon
½ cup water

The Bread Sauce:
1 cup milk
1 small onion with 1 clove stuck in it
1 cup white bread crumbs
1 tablespoon heavy cream—a little more if the sauce is too
    thick for your liking
½ tablespoon butter
salt and freshly ground white pepper to taste

Heat the oven to 400°.

Rub the inside of the chicken very thoroughly with salt and dust with pepper. Fill it with parsley sprigs.

Fold the wings underneath the body—akimbo—and tie the legs together with string to make a neat package. Rub the bird all over with salt. Pour half the lemon juice inside and pat the other half over the outside—gently and thoroughly as if you were patting a cheek. Place it on a rack in a roasting pan, breast up. Add ½ cup of water to the pan to prevent it from scorching. Sprinkle some more salt over the bird. Cook in the center of the oven for 1 hour. Don't open the oven door. There is no need for basting.

Chicken cooked this way has "a good flavour," says Mary Poppins, "and is tender and juicy."

Prepare the bread sauce: Heat the milk with the onion and clove over low heat for 2–3 minutes to bring out the flavours. Stir in bread crumbs and cook gently for 2–3 minutes. Remove the onion and stir in cream and the butter. Season with salt and pepper and serve with roast chicken.

Makes 1 cup or ½ pint.

Shepherd's Pie

2½ pounds ground or minced rump steak or top round
2 small onions
2 tablespoons butter
salt and freshly ground black pepper
juices from the roast beef pan or leftover gravy, bouillon cube,
    or beef stock to moisten the pie
2 pounds potatoes, boiled
finely chopped parsley
ovenproof dish, 10 inches x 7 inches x 2 inches

In a large frying pan or skillet, cook the minced steak for 4–5 minutes, stirring constantly. Turn it into a large bowl. Peel and chop the onions. Add 2 tablespoons of butter to the pan in which the beef was cooked. Cook onions till golden and tender. Mix with the beef. Season with salt and freshly ground black pepper. Add pan juices or gravy to moisten.

Heat the oven to 425°.

Spoon the mixture into the dish. Using a potato ricer, cover the mince evenly with riced potatoes. If you don't have a ricer, spread mashed potatoes with a fork, not pressed down but lightly. Cook in the oven till the potatoes are nicely browned and crisp. Sprinkle with finely chopped parsley before serving.

"This," says Mary Poppins, "is a good way to use up cold roast beef. A dish fit for a king."

Trout

1 trout per person
salt and pepper
flour, about ½ cup
butter, about 1½ tablespoons for each fish
finely chopped parsley
lemons, cut in wedges

Ask the fishmonger to clean the trout for you. Dry the trout thoroughly. Season the inside of each fish with salt and pepper. Spread the flour on a flat plate. Dip each fish into it and shake it to remove the surplus. It should be lightly coated.

In a heavy pan long enough to hold the fish, heat enough butter to cover the bottom to about ⅛ inch in depth. When it foams, add the fish and cook it on one side for 3 minutes. Turn it over and cook for 3 minutes longer. It should be crisp and brown on the outside. Keep it warm in the oven while the others are cooking. When all of them have been cooked, pour off the butter in the pan and add 2 tablespoons of fresh butter. Heat it till foaming and pour over the trout. Sprinkle with finely chopped parsley and serve with wedges of lemon.

"Cooking trout by this method," says Mary Poppins, "takes full advantage of the natural flavour. Lemon juice increases it."

Upside-down Cake
(Topsy-Turvy Cake)

4 tablespoons or $\frac{1}{2}$ stick butter

$1\frac{1}{2}$ cups dark brown sugar

cake tin, 8 inches x $1\frac{1}{2}$ inches

Cream the butter and sugar till smooth. Spread the mixture evenly over the bottom of the cake tin. Set aside.

6 tablespoons butter

$\frac{1}{3}$ cup sugar

2 eggs

1 cup self-rising flour

3 whole peaches, peeled, halved, and pits (stones) removed if fresh

6 cherries, maraschino or glacé

Heat the oven to 350°.

Cream the butter and sugar till light and fluffy. Add the eggs, one at a time, beating vigorously after each one. Add the flour gradually and beat thoroughly. Lay the peaches, cut side down, with a cherry in the "cup," on the prepared cake tin: one in the middle and the other five close to the edge of the tin. This makes a pretty arrangement. Spoon the batter over the peaches and level it off with a spoon. Bake for 45 minutes in the center of the oven.

Loosen the cake round the edge and turn it out on a pretty plate. Pineapple rings, apricots, rhubarb, or apples may be used in place of peaches.

Very Plain Cake

4 tablespoons or ½ stick butter

½ cup granulated sugar

1 egg, separated

¼ teaspoon vanilla extract

1½ cups sifted all-purpose flour

2 teaspoons baking powder

¼ teaspoon salt

½ cup milk

baking tin, 8 inches x 1¼ inches, lightly greased
    and dusted with flour

Heat the oven to 325°.

In a mixing bowl cream the butter till light and fluffy. Add the sugar gradually while mixing. Beat hard. Beat in the egg yolk and vanilla extract. Sift the flour, baking powder, and salt together. Stir into the butter and sugar a little flour and then some milk, beating very hard after each addition. Beat the egg white till it will hold a stiff peak when the beater is lifted from the bowl. Fold the beaten white into the batter, lightly and thoroughly. Spoon into the prepared cake tin. Bake for 25–30 minutes or until a toothpick inserted in the middle comes out clean and dry. Turn out to cool on a wire rack.

Walnut Cake

½ cup (¼ pound) unsalted sweet butter
1 cup granulated sugar
2 eggs, separated
1 cup sifted all-purpose flour (sift first and then measure)
½ cup cornstarch
pinch of salt
2 teaspoons baking powder
½ cup milk
1 teaspoon lemon juice
½ cup chopped walnuts
cake tin, 8 inches x 1½ inches, lightly buttered

Heat the oven to 375°.

Beat the butter and sugar together till light and creamy. Add the egg yolks, and continue beating till thoroughly mixed.

Sift the flour with the cornstarch, salt, and baking powder. Add, spoonful by spoonful, to the egg and butter mixture with a little of the milk between each spoonful. Beat thoroughly after each addition. Add the lemon juice. Stir in the chopped walnuts. Beat the egg whites till stiff but not dry. Fold gently into the batter and spoon into the cake tin.

Bake for 30–35 minutes. Cool for a minute or two and then turn out on a wire rack to cool thoroughly.

XXX
Candy Kisses

1 pound almonds
1 cup powdered milk
1 cup powdered sugar
1 teaspoon almond extract
½ cup milk
additional powdered sugar for coating the kisses

Drop the almonds into a pan of boiling water. Lift them out after 1 minute. When they are cool enough to handle, slip them out of their skins. Grind them very fine in a meat grinder or blender.

Mix the ground almonds, powdered milk, and powdered sugar together. Add the almond extract and milk. Take care not to add all of the milk at one time. Mix together thoroughly and knead with your hands. The dough should be very heavy and slightly sticky. A little more milk may be needed if the dough does not bind. Cover the bowl and chill for 1 hour.

Dust your hands with additional powdered sugar and roll balls of dough, using about 1 teaspoon for each ball. Roll balls in powdered sugar and store in a cool larder or in the refrigerator. There will be about 60 kisses.

"Very nice," says Mary Poppins, "for a special bedtime treat."

Yorkshire Pudding

1 cup flour
pinch of salt
1 small egg
1 cup milk and water in equal parts

Heat the oven to 425°.

Sift the flour and salt into a mixing bowl. Make a well in the middle and drop the egg into it. Add a little of the milk and mix, starting in the center, gradually drawing in the flour while pouring in more milk. Mix thoroughly with an egg beater or whisk and let stand in a cool place for 1 hour.

Heat about 1 tablespoon of the drippings or fat from the roast chicken in an ovenproof pan, about 12 inches x 12 inches. Tip it and tilt it till it is coated with fat. Pour in the batter and bake for 25 minutes. It will be by then well puffed up, crisp, and brown. Mary Poppins cuts it into squares for serving.

Zodiac Cake

1 large egg, separated
2 squares semi-sweet chocolate
1½ cups all-purpose flour
2 teaspoons baking powder
¼ teaspoon salt
4 tablespoons or ¼ cup butter
¾ cup sugar
½ cup ground nuts (walnuts, pecans, or hazels)
1 teaspoon vanilla extract
¾ cup milk
round cake tin, 3 inches x 11½ inches

Heat the oven to 375°.

Grease the cake tin with butter and flour it. Shake out the excess flour. Separate the egg yolk from the white. Melt the chocolate in a small bowl standing in hot water. Sift the flour and measure. Sift again with the baking powder and salt.

Cream the butter—beat it till light and creamy. Add the sugar gradually and continue beating. Add the egg yolk and beat even harder. Stir in the melted chocolate and ground nuts. Stir the vanilla into the milk. Add some flour to the chocolate mixture and then stir in some milk, a little more flour and then some more milk, till both have been used up. Beat very thoroughly.

Beat the egg white till stiff and fold gently into the batter. Pour into prepared pan. Bake for 30 minutes.

Mary Poppins decorates this cake with small silver stars.

 Index

78